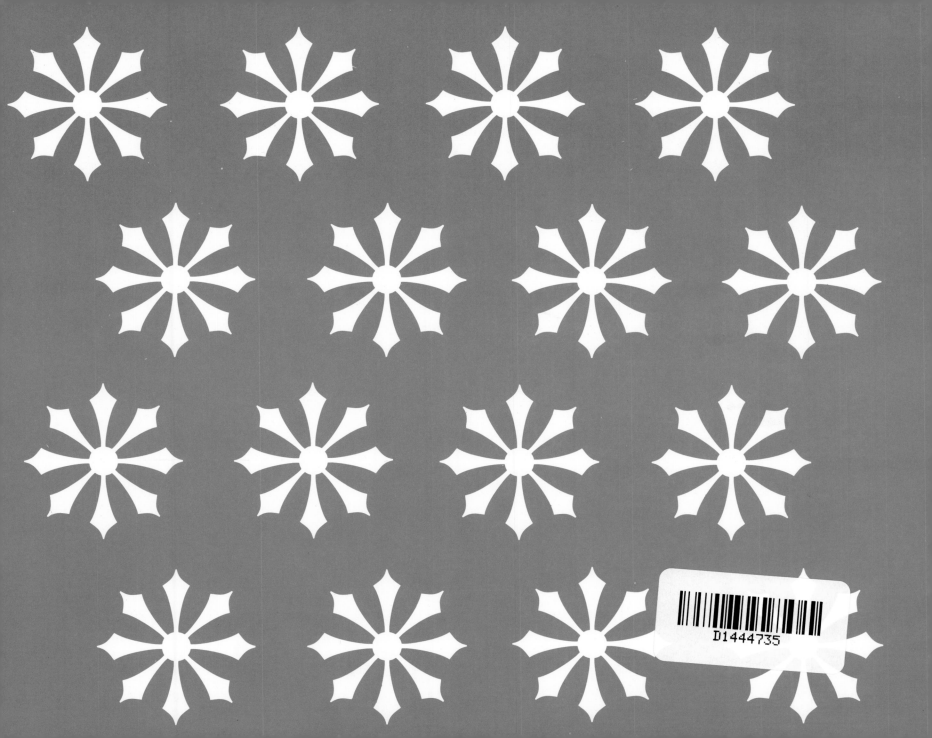

# Jenny and the Hanukkah Queen

## Jean Little

### Illustrated by *Suzanne Mogensen*

**VIKING**

**J**enny loved to draw. She was good at it too. One day she drew a picture of her mother. In the picture, her mother's hair was black and curly. She was very round but not terribly tall. Her eyes danced and she wore a wide, loving smile.

"It looks just like her," said her father.

Usually they taped Jenny's pictures up on the refrigerator but that one was so good her father hung it on the wall.

The day after Halloween, she drew a great picture of her friends Carol and Tema and herself in their costumes. Carol was Red Riding Hood, Jenny was the grandmother and Tema was the wolf.

"The faces are wonderful, Jenny," her teacher said. "Maybe you'll grow up to be a famous artist."

Then Carol's mother took the three girls to the Santa Claus Parade. A clown gave Tema a big smacking kiss and pulled the tassel on Carol's hat. Jenny laughed so hard her stomach hurt.

When Santa Claus came riding by, at the very end, Carol waved and called, "Merry Christmas, Santa."
Jenny did not wave. Tema kept her hands in her pockets.

"Merry Christmas, girls," boomed Santa. "Ho, ho, ho!"

He seemed to be looking straight at Jenny and Tema. Jenny gave a quick little wave. She pulled her hand back down fast. She shot a sideways glance at Tema and saw her hand coming back down too.

"It can't hurt to wave," Tema growled.

"We're just being polite," Jenny said. But she felt funny. She and Tema were Jewish. Their families didn't celebrate Christmas.

After lunch, Jenny began drawing parade pictures. She didn't mean to do Santa Claus, but before she knew it, there he was.

"When I was six, my mother's friend took me to the parade," Jenny's mother said.

"Did you see Santa Claus?" Jenny asked.

"Well, I saw the Santa in the parade. Nobody sees the real Santa Claus. I remember jumping up and down and waving when he went by."

"I waved to him too," Jenny confessed. "But Santa doesn't ever come down your chimney if you're Jewish, does he?"

Jenny's mother scrawled an address on an envelope. She did not write neatly. Black and quick, the words jumped onto the paper. When she had finished, she said, "Who needs Santa Claus when they have the Hanukkah Queen?"

Her mother got up and put on her coat. She seemed to be in a big hurry.

Jenny thought way back to last Hanukkah. She remembered the Hanukkah menorah with its row of shining candles. Her mother had lighted them, every night a new one, and Jenny had loved seeing the light growing brighter and brighter. They had played the dreidel game, and she had been given a little net bag filled with chocolate coins covered in gold paper.

But she could not remember a queen.

"What queen?" she said, running after her mother.

"Stay inside. It's cold. We'll talk about the Hanukkah Queen later," Jenny's mother called. She sped away.

Later that afternoon, Jenny and Tema went over to Carol's house.

"Have you ever heard of the Hanukkah Queen?" Jenny asked. Carol shook her head. "I've heard of the Snow Queen," she said, "and the Queen of England. But not the … what did you say?"

"I know about Hanukkah," Tema said. "That's when we light the candles every night at sunset — and my grandma makes latkes. Mmmm!"

"She makes what?" asked Carol.

"Potato pancakes," Jenny explained.

Tema thought a moment. "I don't remember any queen being part of it," she said at last, thinking hard. "Just some men."

"The Hanukkah Queen," Jenny said cautiously, "is something like Santa Claus, I think, only better. My mother knows all about her. She's special and I'm pretty sure, for her, you have to be Jewish."

Carol looked shocked.

"Nobody's better than Santa Claus," she declared.

"You only say that because you don't know about the Hanukkah Queen," said Jenny.

"My mother will know," Tema put in quickly. "We can ask her when she comes to take us home."

As soon as they were in the car, Jenny asked about the Hanukkah Queen.

"Who told you about her, Jenny?" Tema's mother asked.

"My mother."

"I thought as much," said Tema's mother and she laughed. "It's late, Jenny. Ask your mother to tell you. No, Tema, not now. I'll explain later."

Jenny slammed the car door. Why did everyone say "later"?

At supper, she could not wait another minute.

"Please," she begged her mother, "please tell me about the Hanukkah Queen."

Jenny's father looked at Jenny's mother.

"Do tell us," he said. "We'd both be interested."

Jenny's mother gazed at Jenny. Her cheeks glowed. Her eyes sparkled. Her voice was the one she used for telling stories.

"At the darkest time of the winter," she said, "the Hanukkah Queen comes secretly and leaves gifts for each child who believes in her."

"Is she like Santa Claus?" Jenny breathed.

"A little bit, but she is far more mysterious, more magical and more secret," said Jenny's mother. "You'll never find someone dressed up like the Hanukkah Queen in a mall or on television."

"Does she wear a tall crown?" Jenny wanted to know.

"What do you think?" her mother asked.

"I think she does," said Jenny. "With jewels sparkling in it."

"I think you might be right," said her mother.

"Does she have a sleigh and eight tiny reindeer?"

Jenny's father groaned.

"What do you think?" asked Jenny's mother.

"I don't know," Jenny started to say. Then, into her head, came a picture of a golden chariot that flew.

"Maybe she rides in a golden chariot," she said softly, "that flies without any reindeer. It just flies…"

"That's it exactly," said her mother. "And when children look out their window at night, they sometimes see her passing high above and they think they've seen a shooting star."

Jenny was in bed when the phone rang. She heard her mother laugh.

"Of course I can tell you about the Hanukkah Queen," she said.

She came and shut Jenny's door.

"My mother told me all about the Hanukkah Queen yesterday," Tema said on Monday morning. "My Uncle David is staying with us and he said it was nonsense. He told me the Hanukkah story again about those brothers and how the oil ran out but the lights in the temple kept shining. Then my mom said, 'Don't you remember, David, how we longed for a Hanukkah Queen when we were Tema's age?'"

"What did he say then?" asked Jenny.

"He didn't say one more word," Tema said with a grin. "The Hanukkah Queen is just for children. Anybody would know that."

That day, Jenny began trying to draw the Hanukkah Queen. She drew her shimmering robes. She drew her fur-trimmed train sweeping along the ground behind her. She drew her many-pointed crown with its glowing jewels.

But she could not draw her face. No matter how hard she tried, no face she drew looked magical enough for the Hanukkah Queen.

She gave up and drew the Queen's golden chariot instead, flying through the sky and shining like a star.

The next night she tried drawing the Queen's castle. Her mother loved the castle picture. She wrote "THE HANUKKAH QUEEN'S CASTLE by Jenny" on the bottom in her quick, untidy writing.

"Jenny, let's make a Hanukkah mobile," her mother said.

They made dreidels and Hebrew letters out of dough and baked them in the oven. Then Jenny's mother strung them together and hung the mobile from the ceiling.

At last, Erev Hanukkah, the first night of the festival, was only a few hours away. Jenny's mother got out the menorah and two candles. In the centre, she placed the one she would use to light the other eight. Then she set the first one in its place on the end of the candleholder.

Jenny played with a dreidel.

"Will I hang up my stocking for the Hanukkah Queen to fill?"

"No!" Jenny's mother snapped.

Jenny dropped the dreidel. Her mother's voice softened at once.

"The Hanukkah Queen will find her own way to deliver your gifts. Wait and see."

"Santa Claus brings Carol stacks of boxes," Jenny said.

"The Hanukkah Queen doesn't bring everything in a big heap but you can trust her not to be outdone by an old man in white whiskers," her mother said. "Remember, Jenny, Christmas only lasts one day but Hanukkah goes on for eight."

It was five o-clock. Soon the sun would go down and it would be time to light the first candle. Jenny sat on the couch. She stared up at their mobile. The small tops and curly letters were twirling. Watching them made Jenny feel dizzy. She leaned her head back and closed her eyes.

"Jenny," her mother called. "It's time to light the candles."

Jenny's eyes flew open. Outside the window, the sun was setting. She jumped up and hurried to join her parents. She was almost there when she saw a pile of gifts beneath the window.

"Oh, was the Hanukkah Queen here?" she cried.

"Hush, Jenny," her mother said. But she was smiling.

Then she lit the first candle and murmured the Hebrew words of blessing.

For an enchanted moment, as the bright flame shot out, Jenny completely forgot about the gifts the Hanukkah Queen had brought. In the darkening window-pane, the small shining light was reflected back. It was as though, on the very first night of all, the light of Hanukkah had begun to grow, to drive back the winter night.

Then she opened her presents. Her favourite was a big fairytale book that she had stared at longingly in the bookshop. She opened it in the middle and drank in the luminous pictures of towering beanstalks and merry dwarves, flying boats and gentle unicorns.

The latkes were just as delicious as Tema had said. Mmmm! And at her place lay the gold mesh bag of chocolate coins.

At bedtime, her mother read her the story of Cinderella. When she rose, Jenny held onto her new book.

"Let me look at the pictures one more time," she begged. "I'm not a bit sleepy — and it's Hanukkah."

"All right," her mother said. "Fifteen minutes more."

Jenny opened the book at the very beginning. She noticed, for the first time, the message written in it.

*For Jenny*
*with love from*
*The Hanukkah Queen*

Jenny stared at the untidy black writing for a long time.

The next night, she at last drew the picture she had been trying to draw for so long. In it, the Hanukkah Queen was dressed in splendid robes and she wore a lofty crown. But her hair was black and curly. She was very round and not terribly tall. Her eyes danced. And her face wore a wide, loving smile.

*This book is dedicated to Michele Landsberg who introduced me to the Hanukkah Queen*
*and to Jenny Lewis and Tema Sarrick who let me use their names in my story*

VIKING
Published by the Penguin Group
Penguin Books Canada Ltd, 10 Alcorn Avenue, Ontario, Canada M4V 3B2
Penguin Books Ltd, 27 Wrights Lane, London W8 5TZ, England
Viking Penguin, a division of Penguin Books USA Inc., 375 Hudson Street, New York, New York 10014, USA
Penguin Books Australia Ltd, Ringwood, Victoria, Australia
Penguin Books (NZ) Ltd, 182-190 Wairau Road, Auckland 10, New Zealand
Penguin Books Ltd, Registered Offices: Harmondsworth, Middlesex, England
First published 1995
2 4 6 8 10 9 7 5 3 1
Text copyright © Jean Little, 1995
Illustrations © Suzanne Mogensen, 1995

Printed and bound in Hong Kong
**Canadian Cataloguing in Publication Data**
Little, Jean, 1932-
Jenny and the Hanukkah queen
ISBN 0-670-85268-6
I. Mogensen, Suzanne.   II. Title.
PS8523.I77J4  1995          jC813'.54          C94-932065-X
PZ7.L57Je 1995
British Library Cataloguing in Publication Data Available
American Library of Congress Cataloguing in Publication Data Available